KATHRYN CAVE is a writer who spent her early years
being wilfully misunderstood by her older brother and sisters.
As a result she developed a crew of imaginary friends – wolves, dragons,
aardvarks, trolls – who did exactly what she wanted and were a great
improvement on reality. Kathryn had her first book published in 1984
and since then she has written many books for children including
Something Else, illustrated by Chris Riddell, which was shortlisted for both
the Kate Greenaway Medal and the Smarties Prize and won the first
UNESCO award for Children's literature. Kathryn's other books
for Frances Lincoln include *One Child, One Seed* and *Troll Wood*.

CHRIS RIDDELL is a multi-award winning graphic artist whose
distinctive line drawings appeal to both children and adults alike.
Chris studied illustration at Brighton Polytechnic and has illustrated
many acclaimed books for children of all ages including
The Edge Chronicles and *Jonathan Swift's Gulliver*. In addition to his
children's books work, Chris is a renowned political cartoonist.
He lives in Brighton with his wife and children.

F

FRANCES LINCOLN
CHILDREN'S BOOKS

Frances Lincoln Children's Books,
74-77 White Lion Street, London, N1 9FF
www.franceslincoln.com

First published in 1991 by Frances Lincoln Children's Books
This edition published in paperback in 2013

ISBN: 978-1-84780-480-8

Text © Kathryn Cave 1991
Illustration © Chris Riddell 1991

A CIP catalogue record for this book is available from
the British Library.

1 3 5 7 9 8 6 4 2

Printed in China

Counting Sheep

Kathryn Cave
Chris Riddell

F

FRANCES LINCOLN
CHILDREN'S BOOKS

Last thing at night, when Dad goes round
to switch the central heating down
and put the cat out for the night,
all children should be tucked up tight.

One night Tom wasn't: he had had
three drinks of water from his Dad,
six hugs and four good-nights from Mum,
but even so, sleep wouldn't come.

At 10 o'clock his mum said: "Right.
This is your very last good-night.
I'm off to bed. Just go to sleep –
and if you can't, try counting sheep."

Six sheep ambled through Tom's door
and lay down on the bedroom floor.
They sighed and snuffled, yawned a lot,
then fell asleep – but Tom did not.

The seventh sheep was lean and spry.
It looked at Tom and winked an eye.
Before you could say "Mother Hubbard",
it vanished through his bedroom cupboard.

Beyond the cupboard lay a wood,
deep, desperate and dark. Tom stood
astonished till a fearsome growl
warned him wolves were on the prowl.

Two wolves, four wolves, six, eight, ten –
soon Tom had counted 12 of them.
Their teeth were sharp, their manners free.
Tom judged it best to climb a tree.

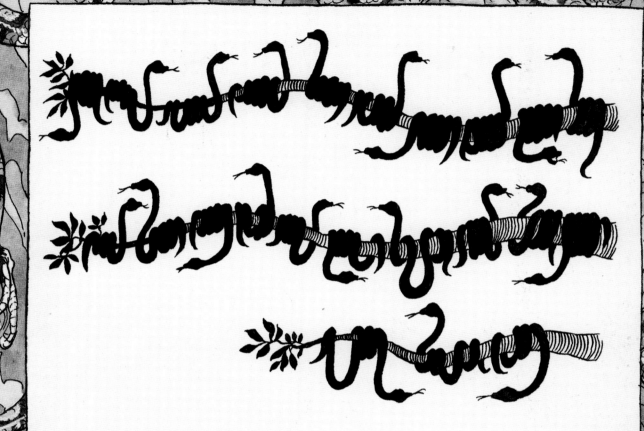

There's no place safer than up high
unless a python should drop by,
for pythons rarely knock or phone
and they don't visit you alone.

Tom counted ten, he counted twenty
(believe me, twenty python's plenty).
He counted 23, and so
I think that he was right to go.

The mountainside was cold and bare.
The wind that whiffled through Tom's hair
brought to his ears a mournful note –
the gentle bleating of a goat.

Some goats are small, some goats are sweet.
Tom's weren't: they had great horns and feet.
When 36 goats cut up rough
one cannot exit fast enough.

Approaching from the east Tom saw
a band of pirates armed for war,
with pistols, cutlasses and axes,
looking for some target practice.

No time to hide, no place to run,
outnumbered 45 to one,
Tom ducked beneath the gangplank fast
and tripped them up as they went past.

The wind grew sharper, Tom grew colder.
Penguins pecked him on the shoulder –
30, 40, 54,
they crowded round to peck some more.

Tom counted west, he counted east.
It didn't change things in the least.
Desperately, as dawn was breaking,
he built an ice raft to escape in.

The beach looked like the perfect spot
for Tom to sunbathe. It was not.
61 enormous bears
seemed to think that it was theirs.

Counting them by twos and fours,
Tom dodged noses, teeth and claws.
I think they only meant to play
but Tom was glad to drive away.

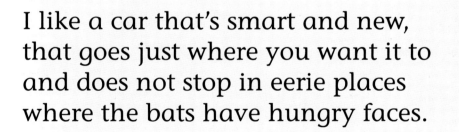

I like a car that's smart and new,
that goes just where you want it to
and does not stop in eerie places
where the bats have hungry faces.

One vampire bat's enough for me.
If you bump into 70,
don't stay to count them up too long:
head for shelter fast, like Tom.

Ghosts are fine in ones or twos,
depending on the sort you choose
(on gloomy Sundays when it's raining
they can be quite entertaining)

but 88 ghosts in a huddle
almost always leads to trouble.
As soon as Tom had finished counting
he dashed out and down the mountain.

Bombay tigers can be kind.
All the same, if you should find
97 in a heap
the best thing is to let them sleep.

And when you're counting them in whispers
please DON'T tread upon their whiskers.
Tigers don't like being woken.
Luckily Tom's door was open . . .

A hundred shadows swoop and fall
across the blankness of Tom's wall.
Tom shut the door, tucked up the sheep,
put out the light, and went to sleep.

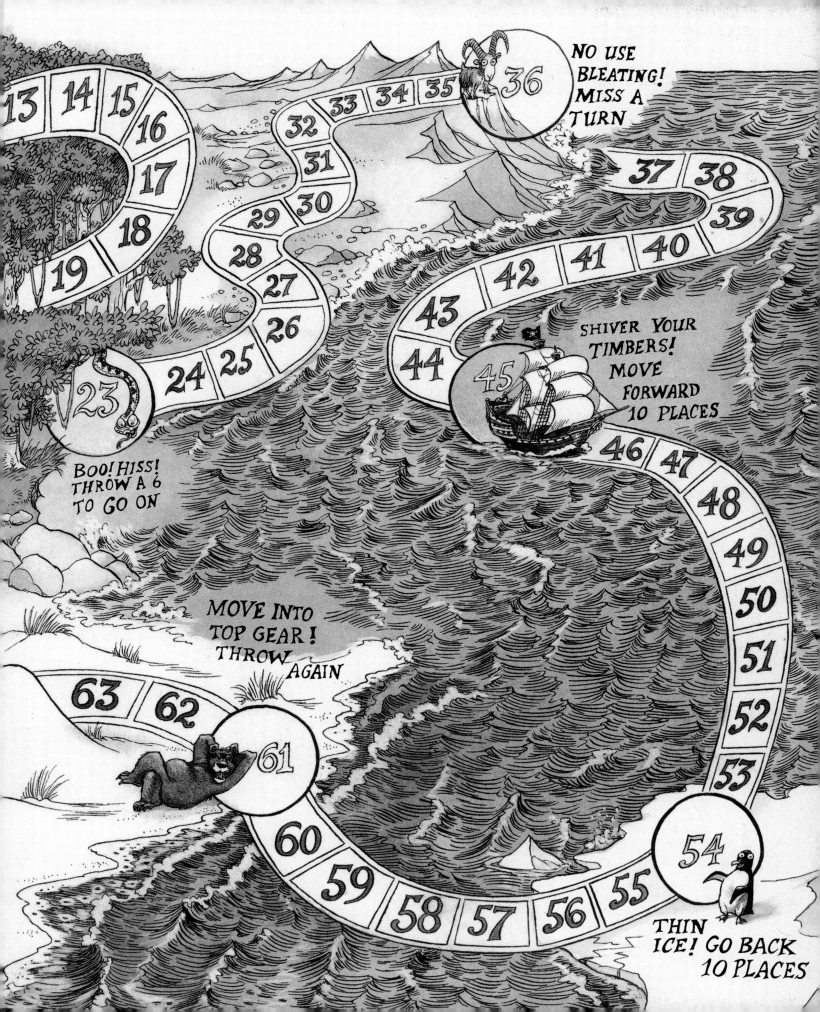

MORE TITLES FROM FRANCES LINCOLN CHILDREN'S BOOKS

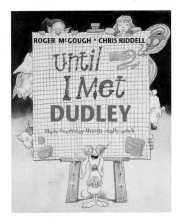

UNTIL I MET DUDLEY
Roger McGough
Illustrated by Chris Riddell

Have you ever wondered how a toaster works?
Or a fridge-freezer, or a washing-up machine?
In this fun-filled book of how things work,
Dudley, the techno-wizard dog, provides the
answers, taking us into a fascinating world
of technology to discover the workings
of familiar machines.

TROLL WOOD
Kathryn Cave
Illustrated by Paul Hess

A family in need of a new home find themselves
forced to take shelter in the mysterious Troll Wood.
But within the wood they find a world of unpicked
flowers, uneaten fruits and unexplored paths,
just waiting to be discovered. Can you see the
trolls in Troll Wood? And will you join them there?

I WANT A PET
Lauren Child

This little girl really wants a pet. But what kind
should she get? After all, lions have a habit of
snacking between meals and boa constrictors are
a little too friendly! Lauren Child's story of a small
girl's search for the perfect pet is sure to delight.

Frances Lincoln titles are available from all good bookshops.
You can also buy books and find out more about your favourite titles,
authors and illustrators on our website: www.franceslincoln.com